F
RIC

THE ... TREE

D1380069

It w...
dau...
beg...
stor...
feet...
a st...
the...
kee...

She...
The...
stra...
wit...
fro...
dea...
oth...
'idi...
boo...
vat...
ded...

The...
ber...
Gla...
the...
Grew and *Twice Times Danger*, as well as stories
for older readers, *The Game, Wolfsong* and *To
Summon a Sp...* ...t lives in London.

Also by Enid Richemont

Enid Richemont

The Time Tree

WALKER BOOKS
AND SUBSIDIARIES
LONDON • BOSTON • SYDNEY

First published 1989 by Walker Books Ltd
87 Vauxhall Walk, London SE11 5HJ

This edition published 1998

2 4 6 8 10 9 7 5 3

Printed in England by Cox & Wyman Ltd, Reading, Berks

British Library Cataloguing in Publication Data
A catalogue record for this book is
available from the British Library.

ISBN 0-7445-6072-1

For Polly and Justine

Chapter One

It was summer.

It was August.

It had been their last year at Primary school and they already sensed that nothing would ever be quite the same again. Perhaps that was why they loved the tree so much.

To Joanna and Rachel, the tree was just like a great house full of rooms.

Their favourite room was the one they called the attic. It was not so very high up, but it was well hidden and quite difficult to reach, and there was only enough space on it for two or, possibly, three people. It was their secret place and they felt quite private about it.

That was why it was so disturbing – the feeling of being watched.

Rachel and Joanna were best friends and they had always thought they could tell each other anything, but this was different. How could you talk about a vague prickling at the back of your neck? How could you admit to a feeling that every word you said, each gesture that you made was being heard, noted and considered by an invisible audience? It simply sounded silly. And a bit childish. Secretly fearful of losing sight of each other among the vast corridors of the huge Comprehensive, they had recently become very wary of their friendship and neither was prepared to take the risk of making a fool of herself.

So they said nothing, but the feeling lay between them just the same — too heavy and oppressive to be ignored. They tried. They really worked at it, sitting astride their branch, swinging their legs and making up unlikely stories about their teachers.

"Wouldn't be surprised if he fancied ... You know ..."

"And what about Miss Hoskins? Did you see that blouse she was wearing?"

And, their thoughts elsewhere, they giggled self-consciously, without much real amusement.

But it was all nonsense, wasn't it? It had to be. This was their secret place and no one could possibly be watching them. To begin with, it would not have been easy for someone to have climbed up much higher. Anyway, no one could have got up that tree without being spotted and they had both been sitting there for ages and ages.

And so they went on eating their chocolate, flicking through the pages of an old magazine, folding a piece of paper into a fortune-telling game and telling outrageous jokes — furiously acting as if nothing at all had changed.

The girl could not take her eyes off them.
She watched them, fascinated but terrified,

not daring to move for fear they would attack her.

The tree was in a wood.

Once it had been a wild wood, which had covered many acres of land. Foxes and badgers had lived in it. Deer and wild pig had been hunted on it. That was a very long time ago. Now the little of it that was left had been tamed and enclosed in a park. Now you could not walk through it without catching glimpses of neatly shaved lawns and richly patterned flowerbeds and, further away, the metallic glint of the swings and slides in the children's playground.

There was a lane that went past the back of the wood. The lane was not supposed to be the entrance to the park. That was some distance away, along streets and through the big, green-painted iron gates. Near those gates was a notice-board, which told you at great length, and in very small print, what you could and could not do in this open space, among these winding paths and smooth lawns, on the round boating lake and the sports field, in the playground and the little wood. Someone had spray-painted a silly face over the words. Nobody minded. Nobody read them anyway.

Behind a tangle of blackberry bushes and stinging nettles lay a broken-down fence. That was the way in for the people who knew about it, for the kids who lived there. That was the real way in.

The girl frowned.

She was puzzled by their blue hose, their loose shirts and their funny white shoes, but they did not fool her with those boy's garments. What were they? Travelling players? For what honest maid, she wondered admiringly, would deck herself out like that? Even the gipsy wenches showed a little modesty.

Of course there was nobody watching them.

So they each began thinking, uncomfortably, that perhaps it was something else that was wrong.

Perhaps something had happened to their friendship. Perhaps they had simply stopped being best friends – people did, after all. These things happened. For they could each think of at least four people whose own parents didn't even live together any more. People could stop loving each other. People could even stop liking each other. Nothing was for ever.

And the whole idea was silly.

They were ten years old, nearly eleven, and pretty sensible, and they knew that no one could possibly be watching them every single time they went to the tree. After all, who

10

would bother? What did they get up to that could possibly attract such undivided attention?

So, maybe, they had come to the sad point where there was nothing further to say and nothing more to share. At that moment this idea was far more disturbing than the remote possibility of someone spying on them.

Suddenly the tree with its attic branch seemed like nothing but childish nonsense and they decided to go home.

They disappeared into a green mist.

The girl watched them go. She was sorry that they were leaving, for they were curiosities and even stranger than herself. Curiosities seldom came her way, but when they did, she found them oddly comforting.

Freaks she had seen at fairs, but these were not freaks. She would have liked to have come closer to them, to have put out a finger and touched their hair, their skin, or the fabric of their clothes, but she dared not. For anything might happen.

Even the people in her own village had been known to attack her, and these were strangers.

Rachel and Joanna walked down the lane.

It was really a country lane, trapped inside the city, where roses, grown wild, ran amok over the tatty fences of neglected gardens, and long-forgotten apple trees dropped their small, wizened fruit to ferment in the gutters. The lane dipped between the dark side walls of two gaunt buildings. Then it opened out, astonishingly, into a street of tall Victorian houses, whose windows were often boarded up and whose porches now bore the names of many occupants. It was a long, boring street, its boredom lessened only by the possibility of a chance encounter with an attention-seeking cat. And today all the cats were inside, or round the back, asleep in the shade.

The two girls crossed the bridge over the railway. The High Street was full of afternoon shoppers, and Rachel and Joanna moved, in a dream-like and oppressive silence, past the exhausted young woman with the screaming infant and the gang of punks, too hot to be aggressive, whose tough masks were already melting in the sun. This was where Rachel lived – in the bottom half of an old house in a leafy suburban street near the shopping centre. Joanna lived one stop away on the tube.

At the turn-off for the station, Jo announced awkwardly, "I really ought to go home now."

"Not coming back to the house, then?" Rachel felt almost relieved.

"Not this time."

"Coming tomorrow, though?" Rachel

asked quickly, suddenly fearful of a refusal.

Jo grinned and nodded, and the tension was instantly broken.

"Half-past two, OK?"

"See you."

Chapter Two

Anne sat under the table, thinking.

At that moment the table marked out the boundaries of her private world, its edges defined by the four carved legs. She played idly with the rushes on the floor, pleating the stems into elaborate shapes or weaving them into little plaits. The summer heat had made them stale-smelling. It would have helped if she had brought in sweet herbs from the garden. That was one of the simple tasks they gave her, for they disapproved of idleness, even in a fool. But it felt so good to be sitting alone in the cool shade of her table house that she did not care.

If her mother had been around, she would have chided her for such infantile behaviour but, happily for Anne, she was not. Today she was far too busy. Anne's older sister, Kate, was to be betrothed, and to no common yeoman either, for Thomas was a lad of noble birth – a Gentleman, no less. At fifteen, Kate, with her smooth, high forehead, her carefully plucked brows and small, delicate mouth, had brought much honour to the family. Thomas had persisted in his courtship in spite of the existence of Kate's lackwit sister, in spite of the muttered warnings from the goodwives of the village, and their father was very proud.

"But she comes of good stock," he boasted, "and she is fair and virtuous. As for Anne — accidents can happen in the noblest families."

Anne sighed. It was sad to be nothing but a burden — a burden and a shame.

Her father, not noticing her, sat down at the table and began to write. Anne knew what he was doing; she had already peeped at the columns of numbers in the big ledger. Honour did not come cheaply and she knew that he was working out the cost of the banquet and the cost of the sewing women, too, for they were all going to look very grand. There was much talk of farthingales and French hoods and starch. Even she, Anne, was to have a special gown, although her mother had sniffed and said that it was good money wasted upon an idiot.

And they reminded her daily that she was to be silent at the feast, to smile modestly but say nothing, lest she shame them.

She squatted, watching the shifting and flexing of the heavy leather boots, aware of her father's concentration and wishing for the impossible — that she could help him a little, for she knew that her existence brought him nothing but woe. And she thought again about the maids in the tree — if maids they were. They were able to write. Many times she had seen them writing things down in their small books. Anne sighed. If only she could write, she thought, she could tell people things. There was much locked away inside her that she wanted to say. But who would waste precious time teaching her?

Wistfully she fingered the lines of the carvings on the table legs, pretending they were letters.

Joanna walked up the hill past the car park. The sky was grey and white. It looked like rain.

She shivered. Would it be the same today?

Over the past few months the differences between herself and Rachel had seemed to grow and little things, which once would not have troubled her at all, had suddenly become irritating. Rachel's family, for instance, always seemed to be so infuriatingly well organized, making her own, by comparison, look totally chaotic. And Jo was always forgetting things, while Rachel never seemed to lose anything at all.

But then people had to be different, didn't they? It would be so boring to have a best friend who was exactly like yourself. And anyway, she liked Rachel. She liked her smooth, fair skin and her blonde hair (trendily cut these days by one of her mum's friends). And she always took Rachel's side whenever she was teased, and suffered with her whenever she started blushing, which she did so readily. (Joanna herself did not get so easily embarrassed.) Suddenly she made up her mind.

I'm going to say something, she thought, about the feeling of being watched. I know it's going to sound silly but I'm going to say it just the same.

She dawdled past the Indian fabric shop with its shimmering saris and the charity shop with its wire baskets full of exciting jumble. Sometimes they bought clothes there. They would pool their pocket money and come away with their loot – a velvet jacket, threadbare but interesting; a crumpled T-shirt with an unusual slogan or, once, a sequinned and gold-threaded skirt that someone might have worn to a fancy dress party and then discarded. And they shared everything because that way they each had twice as much.

Joanna was late.

Rachel was waiting.

She had been waiting for some time, nervously, not even certain any more that Jo would turn up. Occasionally she would stand on tiptoe, trying to pick out Joanna's ginger bunches from among the crowd and quickly ducking down again to make herself inconspicuous. Waiting for people made her feel self-conscious. She hated it.

And she began thinking, all over again, about the previous afternoon. She remembered the heat and the prickly feeling that someone was watching them. They couldn't go through all that again today.

She came to a decision.

I'm going to tell Jo, she thought. It's going to sound crazy but I'm going to tell her just the same.

But when they saw each other they were so relieved that they hugged and forgot everything.

"What have you brought?" asked Rachel.

"Just some money; didn't have time for anything else. Thought we'd go to your big supermarket."

"OK."

They walked up the street arm in arm, as if nothing had ever been wrong.

Rachel's big supermarket was the kind of place that sold everything – even parasols and garden chairs. It was the kind of supermarket you could lose people in, and they did, several times. Soon, the soppy, sentimental music began to make them feel giggly and they started to fool around, dancing down the long, almost empty aisles.

When they came upon the trayful of Special Offer Outsize Bras, it was simply too much. They picked over voluminous lace-trimmed constructions in tea rose or baby blue and held them against their chests.

"Mine's bigger than yours!"

"Mine's D-cups — look!"

"Well mine's F-cups!"

"That's nothing . . . mine's Z-cups."

A woman glared at them disapprovingly, which only made them choke and splutter with laughter.

Sobering up with difficulty they managed somehow to put together a couple of cans of Coke, some chocolate bars and a few packets of crisps before staggering out into the street, still nudging each other and giggling.

But halfway to the park they suddenly became serious.

"Listen," said Joanna boldly, "I think someone was watching us — yesterday afternoon, when we were up in the tree. I mean, there wasn't anybody around but I could sort of — feel it. Look, I know this sounds silly . . ."

"No, it doesn't," Rachel said quickly. "I was going to say exactly the same thing to you."

It was out at last, and they both felt better.

"What shall we do," asked Joanna, "if it happens again today?"

They each thought about it.

"Challenge them," said Rachel at last. She sounded quite angry.

"How?"

"Call out. Yell. Tell them we know they're there and then see what happens."

They went on up the lane. A boy came skateboarding towards them, twisting his shoulders in an arrogant gesture, showing off. When he drew level with them, he pulled a face at Joanna and mouthed, "Ginger!"

They ignored him.

At the top of the lane they ducked under the fence into the wood. And there was their tree. They climbed it defiantly. No one was going to spoil this afternoon.

Anne always felt proud of herself for being able to find the right place each time. After all, there were plenty of saplings in the forest and one looked much like another. A fool and an imbecile she might be, but she knew how to read her path from the shape of a bush, a scattering of yellow-lipped comfrey or a beech stump smothered in ivy.

And now she had her reward.

For the maids were there.

Oh but she had waited so long.

She supposed that she must be brave, too, for she knew that not everyone would have dared venture as deep into the forest as this. Rogues' and vagabonds' country, people called it, but that did not trouble Anne. Any place beyond the safety of her own garden walls could be dangerous for someone like her.

She knew that she was a freak. She knew

that her presence offended people, that her shadow falling on the wooden pails might sour the milk, that even her passing might cause one or two of the old women to make the sign against the Evil Eye before turning their heads away.

But it was the children she feared the most.

For she could never tell when they were creeping up behind her until her hair was painfully tweaked, or a stone was lobbed. And then they would snigger behind their hands and mime the noises that she made when she tried to protest.

"Moo! Moo! Moo!"

"Wallawallawalla!"

But the forest was kind. It offered her no harm.

The brambles didn't pick on Anne because she was different: they would have scratched anybody. And as for vagabonds, she had never seen one.

She had only seen two strange maids up in a tree.

Rachel and Joanna sat on the high branch, listening. Not talking. Listening.

"It's happening again," whispered Joanna.

Rachel nodded.

"Ssh!" she said. "Let's see if they give themselves away."

So they sat, absolutely still. Listening.

A twig snapped somewhere above their heads. They looked up sharply. Bits of twig and tree droppings scuttered through the leaves. A pigeon flapped noisily and rose into the air.

"They're up there!" Rachel said. Her face was pale and her mouth felt tight and stiff. She was not often angry, really angry, but she was angry now. Something very precious to both of them was being ruined by this stupid game played by some yobbo who obviously had nothing better to do.

"Let's tell them," she said, and she began shouting. "Come on down! We know you're up there!"

But there was no response. No one shouted insults back at them. No one pelted them with orange peel or sweet papers or chewing gum. There was no sound but the rustling of leaves and the distant voices of the little kids in the playground.

Rachel stood up, holding on to the trunk.

"I'm coming up to get you!" she yelled.

Joanna was horrified.

"Rache, you're not serious! The branches up there could be really brittle. It's a very old tree."

But Rachel's mouth was set in a hard line.

"They managed it!"

"We don't know, do we?" said Joanna desperately. "We don't know for sure. There's probably no one up there at all."

But Rachel had already started climbing and she could do nothing to stop her. A touch might have meant disaster. She felt helpless and frightened.

Chapter Three

To the watcher they were a source of perpetual amazement. Maids they undoubtedly were, and nearly grown – about the same age, in fact, as herself; yet they clambered about in the tree like a couple of lads. They even dressed like boys. Her mother, she knew, would have thought them immodest and probably wicked, which was partly what made them so attractive.

She was watching the one with the shorn blonde hair and the round fair cheeks climbing further up the tree. Impressed by her daring, Anne feared at the same time for her safety. Higher up, the branches were thinner and some of them looked brittle. It was not safe. She would surely fall.

Under Rachel's weight, the stout-looking branch unexpectedly creaked.

Shocked, she grabbed at the solid trunk, digging her nails into the rough bark. Down below, too far down, she saw Joanna's frightened face.

"I'm OK!" she called out, but she did not feel it.

The trick, she told herself, was to climb just a little at a time and not to look down. She bravely hauled herself up to the next fork. It was a big tree, wasn't it? There were plenty of footholds and she could always climb down some other way. Besides, she was angry: she was not going to give up now.

"I'll get you!" she yelled, to keep up her spirits, but the only response was the faint droning of a distant aircraft.

Suddenly the wood she was standing on cracked, sending a shower of splinters pattering through the leaves like heavy raindrops. Instantly her right arm shot up and found a small overhead branch which dipped and swung.

Anne could have told her that the branch was going to break. Anne could see that the wood was rotten – the sudden crack came as no surprise at all. She had learnt quite a lot, trotting curiously after her father as he tended the trees on his land, watching him prodding and poking them and pruning away at the dead wood. But this tree was in a forest and had never been cared for.

And already the girl's grip was weakening. Sooner or later, she was bound to fall.

Anne could not see the ground, but she guessed that it must be a long way down. The maid would surely be killed, she thought, or, far worse, crippled – like the boy in the village who sat all day, watching with bitter, old-man's eyes while the other children played.

The red-haired one had begun to climb now, shakily, trying to help her friend – oh, but she would only make things worse.

Anne could see that it was useless. She clenched her fists in a rage: she did not want that maid to fall but she did not know how to stop it from happening. What could she do? What did she know of tree-climbing?

Why, she could not even be sure that what she was seeing was really there. How could it be? A tender sapling with its first slender branches and a great oak gnarled with age occupying the same space? That could not be.

Even a poor fool like Anne could see that.

Rachel clung to the branch with one hand, not daring to move, too mindless with terror even to reach up with her other arm. The sharply-ridged bark scraped against her flesh and made her fingers sting. She felt her fingers slipping. She was going to fall. She knew she was going to fall.

Just inches below her feet was a swelling in the trunk, a solid foothold, but Rachel could not see it.

All she could see was a small red beetle moving slowly, slowly, across a green leaf, like a speck of dust. Time seemed to be running down. Time, for her, she knew, was about to stop altogether.

Anne kicked off her wooden shoes and bunched her skirts in a knot around her hips.

She had to do something.

Joanna could see the foothold.

"Rache, move your right foot down a bit. Your *right* foot, Rachie! There's a place just below you."

Rachel waved her left foot about aimlessly, treading air.

Joanna could not bear it any longer.

She clambered fearfully up the next bit of tree, squeezing the trunk with her knees and digging her toes into the bark, but when she reached out, her fingertips just missed the rubber of Rachel's plimsolls.

There was something solid beneath Anne's feet and she did not waste any time questioning its reality.

For she could see quite clearly now what had to be done, and she could do it.

It was easy.

She was just below the fair girl, behind the curve of the tree. Her left arm was wrapped around its trunk, and her bare toes curled over the tickly bark of a stout branch.

With her right arm she reached out and guided the waving foot to a temporary harbour. Then, as the girl dropped heavily, she grabbed her, supporting her round the waist and hauling her to safety.

Then the red girl took over.

It was extraordinary.

Suddenly someone was there and it wasn't Joanna. Someone was helping, holding Rachel, guiding her down. Rachel caught a glimpse of curly brown hair fringing a white lace cap. Intense dark eyes seemed to meet her own — brown eyes under dark lashes.

But a fancy collar and piled-up skirts still made Rachel think ungratefully: what silly clothes.

Then the vision was gone and she couldn't make it come back. She could see nothing now but Joanna's white face. "It wasn't me," Joanna was saying. "I tried but you wouldn't listen. I didn't help you — it was her ... some girl in fancy dress."

"I know," Rachel said quietly. "I saw her too."

"Then where did she go?"

Rachel shook her head.

"I don't know but she probably saved my life."

"But why ...? How could she ...?"

"I don't know ... I mean, she just sort of ... vanished. I mean, I tried to say something but she just wasn't there any more."

They were both still shocked. They each wanted to go home.

With unusual caution, they scrambled shakily to the ground. It was beginning to rain. They ducked under the fence and hurried down the lane. They did not speak much, for the appearance of the strange girl in the tree was still bothering them.

The horror of Rachel's climb seemed less vivid now than the memory of those dark, frightened eyes.

The slip had been nothing, really: it could have happened to anybody. They agreed not to mention it at home. Parents flapped.

But the girl ...

She was a mystery.

They couldn't have made her up.

If they had both seen her, then she had to be real.

Chapter Four

The weather turned wet and for the next few days Rachel and Joanna did not see each other. Rachel went to a film with her older sister. Jo baked a cake and quarrelled with her brother. They quarrelled because the weather had kept them both indoors and they were sick of the sight of each other. Mark fooled about with a guitar and played records very loudly, which irritated Jo. Jo watched television and made a lot of silly phone calls, which irritated Mark. Then they each said some extremely unpleasant things. Finally Jo had had enough. She slammed the front door and ran out into the rain to walk off a combination of rage and hurt feelings.

While she was out walking, she began to think yet again about Rachel's climb and about the strange girl in the tree. The girl bothered her: how on earth had she done it? One minute she had been there and the next she had simply vanished. It suddenly occurred to Jo that it might have been the girl who had been watching them – that would explain why she had disappeared so promptly. Disappeared? The word made Jo feel vaguely uneasy. Disappeared was silly. People didn't disappear, like rabbits into a conjuror's hat. She had just slipped down through the leaves and run away.

But with all those floppy skirts?

That evening she rang Rachel.

"I wonder why she picked on us, then?" said Rachel. "I mean, there's nothing unusual about us, is there? And what about her? I mean, did you see her clothes? Weird ..."

They both giggled.

A second later they stopped, feeling guilty. Whatever she had been doing and however she was dressed, she had saved Rachel's life.

"Perhaps she was lonely," said Joanna thoughtfully. "She didn't seem to be with anyone."

"I'd really like to see her again," said Rachel. "I ought to thank her anyway."

On the following day the sun came shining out of a cloudless sky, as if it had never rained at all. Frayed tempers were miraculously mended and people queued in the street to buy ice-cream. Mothers gratefully made sandwiches and directed their restless offspring towards parks and swimming pools. Rachel's mother had meant to take the two girls for a picnic on Hampstead Heath, but at the last minute the car wouldn't start.

"You could," she suggested, "take the sandwiches over to the park."

Rachel groaned.

"Let's not go to the park," she said. "It'll be full of little kids."

31

But they did, and it was.

Half a dozen small boys were playing noisy war-games all over their tree. The girls gave up and walked out on to the grass to eat their picnic. Afterwards they lay flat on their backs, like everyone else, rolling up their jeans to brown their legs. They turned over, pushing up their T-shirts in order to toast their backs. They leafed through magazines and dozed. Ladybirds and small insects scuttled over their hands.

At the end of the afternoon they stood up, their hair full of bits of grass, and sleepily wandered over to the tree. The boys had long since gone home.

Cautiously, Rachel and Joanna climbed on to one of the lower branches and sat there, swinging their legs.

The festivities had gone on for two days and the preparations for much longer.

They wanted to impress, but they were not a wealthy family. It was Mother who had rushed, pink-faced and sweating, from supervising the making of the great pies and ornamental jellies to check on the fit of the girls' dresses; who came with damp and spice-smelling fingers to flatten Anne's unruly curls beneath the richly embroidered cap and who fussed as much over the correct starching of their ruffled collars as over the niceties of mounting the peacock on the spit so that, later, its unsinged tail could be spread open at the table like a great jewelled fan.

Anne moved about, stiff and awkward in her new clothes – an open gown of fox-brown brocade trimmed with black and a long turquoise petticoat – like a starched and ruffled doll, who smiled but never spoke, for if she had opened her mouth she would have shamed them all.

Unlike her graceful sister, all dimpled smiles and modest blushes, Anne was not a child to be proud of, and she knew it. She knew, too, that she was lucky to have survived to the age of eleven, for she would always be a burden to her family and would never marry. A child who could only make noises like the beasts in the barn was like something from a menagerie; she was a freak, a monster – possibly even a witch. Why, even the wet-nurse who had fed her as a baby had been known to declare openly that it would have been better if she had not lived.

Perhaps she was a witch and those wanton maids in the tree were her familiars, her evil spirits. At the end of two days of primping, posing and pretending, Anne was exhausted and did not care; better to have friends who were evil than no friends at all.

Unnoticed, she slipped out of the house, rustled through the kitchen garden and, moving slowly in her heavy skirts, crossed the meadow and entered the wood.

It was the same feeling again. They both had it. They were being watched.

"Do you think it's her?" whispered Rachel.

Joanna nodded.

"What do we do? Call her?"

Joanna shook her head.

"If it's her, she'll be too shy. Maybe," the idea suddenly came to her, "she's some sort of refugee and doesn't speak any English." She sighed. "I don't know what we do."

They sat in silence, thinking.

Then Rachel said, "This is going to sound a bit silly but could we will her to come out? Like the time we all willed Miss Shelton to drop the chalk."

Jo giggled.

"And she did," she said. "We could try."

At the beginning they could do nothing at all. They kept on catching one another's eyes and laughing. Then, gradually, the game became more serious.

Come out! they thought. Come out! Come out!

And come she did.

Anne did not enjoy being the focus of other people's attention, and she could always tell when it was happening.

She did not have to watch lips making words. Someone had been calling her. She had felt it. She was sure of it.

No one was going to creep up on Anne.

She turned round to catch them.

Then something extraordinary happened.

For there she was, sitting on the branch of that big old tree, and she had no idea how she got there. Leaves brushed against her cap, and her feet in their new little pointed shoes were swinging in the air.

And the two maids were so real and so close that – if she had dared – she could have reached out a finger and touched them.

She came very gently. Brown eyes blinked through the leaves, then a pale face formed around them, like smoke. Her dark curls had been scraped back under an embroidered cap and the pleated lace ruff round her neck made her head look like the centre of a flower. Her ridiculous skirts – golden-brown and tur-quoise – swelled around her like a ball-dress or something from a Christmas pantomime, the rich fabric caught up in places by twigs. Her thin hands, emerging from narrow, white-ruffed sleeves, were twisting nervously in her lap.

Rachel and Joanna stared at her in open amazement.

At last Jo said, hesitatingly, "Are you part

of a theatre group or something?"

Neither of them wanted to consider any other explanation.

The red girl was speaking to her.

Anne watched the red girl's lips very carefully. She had taught herself to do this when she was still very little, so that strangers did not notice, sometimes, that she was deaf.

She picked out the word "theatre".

Of course. That was the explanation. She smiled – no devils these, but masquers, mummers, come to perform on the village green. Tumblers, perhaps – that would explain their strange costume.

The girl had smiled but she was clearly nervous; her fingers plucked at the fabric of her skirt.

They tried to reassure her.

"I think your dress is very beautiful," said Rachel. The ruff made her think of pictures of Elizabethan clothes she had seen at school, and she added tactlessly, "Is it very old?"

Anne understood. Anne was offended. Anne was furious. Old? Her gown? When her father had just spent a small fortune on their clothes?

Automatically she protested, forgetting, as she frequently did, that her mouth would not make words like other people's.

Chapter Five

It was a language, but not foreign.

They could even pick out one or two words which might have been a funny kind of English.

The girl was trying to tell them something and they couldn't understand: no wonder she looked cross.

The odd thing was, it reminded Joanna of something – something she had heard not so very long ago.

If she had been able, Anne would have left at that moment, run away, gone back to her forest and her sapling, but she seemed to have no choice.

In some mysterious way, the two girls had called her and held her. Why? Were they restless? Did they need a fool to amuse them?

She watched their faces, waiting, like a dog accustomed to abuse, to see what they would do. She waited for them to snigger and point their fingers at their heads and mouth insults. At least there were no stones for them to throw, and acorns did not hurt so much.

But they did nothing.

Perhaps they were frightened of her.

Perhaps, when they had recovered from their shock, they would climb down and run away, making the cross sign against the Evil Eye as they ran.

Joanna remembered now.

She nudged Rachel.

"St James's?" she whispered.

"Oh. Yes. Could be . . ."

Last term, their teacher had taken a small group of them to visit a school for deaf children. They had learned that these children, because they could not hear the sounds that other people made, had never had words to copy when they were very little. They couldn't, without help, even hear the sounds they made themselves, so that their words seemed to come out all wrong. But, like everyone else, they wanted to talk, and talk they did, chattering away like monkeys. And if you gave them time, if you really listened, really concentrated, you could begin to understand what they were trying to say.

Could it be? Was it possible that this girl had the same problem?

"Listen. I'm going to try something," said Joanna.

Feeling very silly (it was only a guess and she might be wrong), she opened her mouth and let out an ear-piercing shriek.

The girl neither blinked nor flinched. It was obvious that she had heard nothing at all.

"You were right, then," said Rachel. "Clever old Jo!"

The two of them felt instantly protective. No wonder, then, that the girl was shy, that she disappeared whenever people were around. She was probably desperately lonely. And maybe she did herself up in all that fancy dress in order to draw attention to herself. After all, if you couldn't hear anything, it might be difficult to believe you were there at all.

When Joanna touched the girl, gently, on the shoulder, she felt her stiffen. She addressed her carefully, remembering to flex her lips as she spoke.

"I'm Jo," she said. She pointed to Rachel. "Her name's Rachel."

She picked up the exercise book in which they wrote down odd, private thoughts and things they didn't want to share with other people, and she unzipped her pencil case and took out a shiny ballpoint pen.

"Will you write your name for us?" She offered the pen and the book – open at an empty page.

The girl took the things warily, as if they might bite, and sat, looking at them, turning them over and over in her hands, and examining them minutely, as if she had never seen anything like them before.

Rachel and Joanna watched her. They were

puzzled. The pen was cheap and ordinary. An exercise book was just an exercise book. What kind of home did this girl come from? Obviously she wasn't putting on an act.

For that matter, what kind of parents would send her out dressed like that?

"Maybe she's some sort of gipsy," whispered Rachel. "The clothes look ... sort of ... real."

But Joanna didn't care.

After all, she was just a girl. She looked about ten, maybe eleven. She could have been in their class at school.

"Look," she said. She took the exercise book out of the girl's hands and brought out some felt-tipped pens. Carefully, she drew pictures of the two of them — Rachel with her sleek, short hair in bright yellow, and herself with a russet pony tail tied back with blue-beaded elastic.

When she had finished, she labelled one RACHEL and the other JOANNA. Then she said the names aloud, taking care over moving her lips.

Anne could not believe it.

They did not find her evil or frightening.

They did not think her a fool.

It had to be a dream but it did not feel like one. If it was a dream then she wanted to go on dreaming it for ever.

At first the two maids had been so unreach-
able that it had felt quite safe to pretend that
they were her friends.

But now they really were.

She stared at them, puzzled. Could they not
see what the others saw? What kind of people
would not think of her as evil, or else a poor
fool to mimic and torment? From where had
these maids come? What village? What town?
What ... other place?

If it were hell itself, she thought defiantly,
she would go there willingly.

She picked up the writing stick the red girl
was offering her and she drew another girl on
the next page, a maid whose new leather
shoes made two neat little points below her
modest skirts. It was the first time she had
ever made a drawing and she held the pen
clumsily in her fist, like a very young child.

She pointed to the picture, and back to
herself.

"Anne," she said.

The girl said, "Aah."

She had to be saying her name.

Rachel came out with the only girl's name
she could think of with the single sound Aah.

"Anne?"

The girl smiled delightedly. Her smile had
an unexpected radiance, like sun coming out
of cloud. Her whole face changed.

Then Rachel took the notebook and wrote underneath the girl's drawing A–N–N–E.

"That right?" she asked.

Anne frowned.

"That's your name, isn't it? Anne?"

The girl stared at the letters, fascinated.

"Aah," she said, and nodded.

Rachel was curious. She handed Anne the pen.

"You do it now," she said.

Anne stared at her and shook her head. People did not usually try to teach letters to fools except in jest.

It was clear to Rachel that the girl did not even know how to write.

"Go on," she said. "Try . . ."

Were they laughing at her, Anne wondered. She would show them.

She studied the shapes of the letters, the straight lines joining at sharp angles. She thought about the carvings on the linen chest, which she had so often traced with her finger; they were much more complicated than this.

With the greatest concentration, she carefully copied the letter A.

"That's good," said Joanna.

"That's super," said Rachel. "You've made an A. A for Anne. A for apple."

Encouraged by their approval, Anne copied out the rest of the word. Then she wrote it again. And again. Each time it became easier.

"Try my name now," said Joanna. "That's much more difficult." And she wrote it out. J–O and J–O–A–N–N–A, for Anne to copy.

Anne stopped looking for reasons and explanations. She was enjoying herself and she just wrote. She wrote A–N–N–E and J–O and R–A–C–H–E–L, over and over again. Sometimes she made mistakes, but when she did, the others were not angry or scornful – they just giggled. Then one of them would guide her hand and she would get it right.

It was like a game. Anne had never played a game, for no one would play with her.

Rachel suddenly looked at her watch. Anne noticed it for the first time and stared at it, her eyes round with amazement.

It was getting late.

"We've got to go home," Rachel said.

"Where do you live?" asked Joanna, suddenly awkward.

What a silly question.

"Why, here, of course."

Rachel asked an even sillier one.

"Where's here?"

Here? Why, Finchley village – where else could it be? Finchley village, not a day's ride from the great city of London where the Queen lived.

And her fingers curled around the slender young limb of a sapling.

And the great tree had gone.

In shocked silence, Rachel and Joanna packed up their things.

"She really was there, though, wasn't she?" said Rachel at last. "I mean, we couldn't both have imagined her, could we?"

Joanna was thinking about it. She was thinking hard.

They climbed down the tree and began walking home.

"We both saw her," Joanna said at last. "We both touched her. She was real."

"But she just disappeared. I mean, she disappeared like a..." She didn't want to say it but she made herself. "Like a ghost. And those clothes ..."

"They weren't a gipsy's."

"They were real, though."

"Yes I know."

They had turned the corner and walked halfway up the road before Rachel said it.

"I thought ghosts always wore white things. I thought they were transparent."

"There is a sort of transparency about her," said Jo. Then she added boldly, "Anyway, I think she's pretty. I think she's beautiful and I don't care."

Chapter Six

She remembered most of the letters, and all the important ones. A–N–N–E made Anne. Her name.

The next afternoon she grubbed around in the garden for a chalking stone and across the dark timber frame of the house, around the side where she hoped no one would notice, she tried out an A. Then, boldly, she added two Ns and an E, and suddenly there it was – ANNE – standing out clear against the brown wood. It made her feel real, seeing her own name in letters: ANNE – no one could ignore that.

She stepped back to admire her work. A–N–N–E. All stick letters, she thought, and no curlicues; it looked very plain. With great daring, she tried out an embellishment or two, like the ones she had seen in broadsheets and manuscripts – a squiggle here, a curly leaf-shape there.

When she had finished, she felt quite proud of herself.

Joanna and Rachel developed an unexpected interest in historical costume for, as Joanna had to admit, with awe, "It isn't *where* she comes from – it's *when*."

So they pored over reference books in the

library and found that dresses like Anne's had been quite ordinary in the sixteenth century.

"The sixteenth century?" Rachel gasped, and held up four fingers.

"Four hundred ..." she whispered.

"Doing a school play?" asked the librarian, curious.

"Might be ..." They exchanged glances and giggled.

Silly kids, thought the woman frostily. Probably up to some mischief – better keep an eye on them.

"Four hundred," repeated Rachel as they sat down at one of the polished tables, and Joanna let out an impressed whistle before clapping her hand over her mouth.

The woman at the desk frowned.

"Sssh!" she said. These two were trouble: she had known it the minute they had come through the door.

"Shakespeare ..." whispered Jo. "I mean, she might actually have seen him."

"Quiet *please*!" snapped the librarian.

"And imagine not being able to read or write at her age, though. Didn't they teach them?"

"Probably thought she was a loony."

"Well she isn't."

The woman stood up. Her spectacles, on a thin gold chain, winked at them malevolently from the frilly shelf of her chest.

46

"If I have to speak to you two again it will be to tell you to leave. This is a study area, not a playground. Look at the notice." The words SILENCE PLEASE were printed in large letters on a glossy card pinned to the wall. "Can't you read?"

This was too much!

Faces pink, they rushed outside, to collapse into giggles downstairs.

Anne went back to the forest the very next day. She wanted to show off to her two friends, persuade them, perhaps, to come with her to admire her letters, but the sapling stubbornly refused to change. She wondered if she had found the right place. It felt right, and she had followed all the signs – anyway, how could she not know her own special little tree?

The next day she tried again, but it was still the same. Then she began to wonder if – wanting friends so badly – she had just made them up. Perhaps she was as lunatic as they thought her.

But the letters were real enough.

And she had already tried out some of the others – a J and an O and an R (that one had been difficult). And a C.

Kate, already playing the goodwife, the mistress of a household, found her covering the beams and even some of the red bricks with chalk marks.

"Oh Anne!" she chided. "What foolery is this?"

Then she looked more closely.

"Why, Anne," she exclaimed. "You have been making letters! Who could have had the patience to instruct you?"

She went off at once to tell Mistress Latymer.

"My poor fool making letters?" cried her mother, shaking her head in total disbelief. "The very idea! She can't even say her own name." Nevertheless she ran out into the garden to see.

But when Anne became aware of the fuss she was causing, she fled in embarrassment.

"How," Rachel casually asked her mother, who worked in a nursery school and might well be expected to know such things, "do you teach kids to read and write?"

"Same way as you were taught ... lots of pictures with words underneath them so you learn the words for things ... alphabet books ... big letters. Why?"

"Oh just wondering."

"How," Joanna asked her mother, "would you teach someone as old as me to read and write?"

"Do you know someone like that?"

"Not really."

48

They spent the following few days preparing for their next visit to the park – reading, collecting things, putting things together. In the Oxfam shop they found an alphabet book, brightly coloured and full of animal pictures. Joanna's brother was scornful.

"Just about your level," he commented.

They rummaged through their own bookshelves for forgotten treasures of their infancy. Rachel's mother was amused.

"Having a second childhood, you two?"

"That's right," said Rachel.

Anne tried yet again.

Tucking up her skirts, she ran through the kitchen garden which was heady with the fragrance of summer herbs, and slipped unnoticed through the gate. She crossed the meadow where dreamy cows stood deep in buttercups and clover.

And where the meadow ended, the forest began.

Rachel and Joanna met with a feeling of suppressed excitement.

The plastic bags they had brought held an odd collection of things: an alphabet and several picture books for very small children; an old-fashioned infants' school text book with funny-looking people drawn on yellowing pages; a couple of cheap sketching pads and exercise books and an amazing assortment of pens and coloured pencils.

It was a day grey with cloud, and chilly for mid August. They were counting on the weather to keep the kids away from the park. When they got there the tree was empty. They sighed with relief and began to climb.

She ran to the place where the sapling stood.

From the moment she touched it, she could feel them calling her: Anne ... Anne ...

And she looked up into the great tree where the two girls sat, swinging their legs.

"Anne!" they were saying. "Anne! Come out! Come and play with us! Anne."

And she came.

There she was, sitting on the branch beside them.

"She's come!" said Jo delightedly. "Oh, Anne, we thought we'd never see you again!"

They looked at her. She was wearing a grubby blue gown, very different from her previous grand dress with its heavy skirts. Her bare feet were dirty and her curls spilled out from under her white cap.

She said, "I have been making the letters you taught me. I have made good progress—see."

The words were garbled but their meaning became clear when she reached for the notebook and pen.

A–N–N–E she wrote, and J–O and a back-wards R. She watched their faces anxiously.

They praised her lavishly.

"Good, Anne, good! Very good! Fantastic. You're really clever!"

Then they got down to the serious business.

They opened the alphabet book. Anne looked at it in amazement. The one or two printed books she had seen had been in black and white. This was bright with colour – who had illuminated it? And it seemed to be writ-ten for children, but what over-indulged child would own such a treasure? Surely no one less than a prince? She put out a hand and touched the fabric of Rachel's jeans. It felt rough, like the clothes of peasants and there were patches on the knees. How any wander-ing player – which, in faith, these probably were – could possess a book of any kind astonished her, but a book specially made for children? They had probably stolen it. She did not care: they were her friends. She stroked the paper reverently.

Joanna turned to the first page.

"Look, Anne," she said, "an ape. A is for ape. The ape in question swung merrily from a tree branch, waving a banana.

"Write it down," ordered Rachel. "Go on ..."

And write it she did, forming the letters with painstaking care.

"B is for butterfly. C is for cat ..." They went slowly through the book, turning the pages. "G is for giraffe." Anne's eyes grew large.

"Monster," she said.

"No, giraffe." They were beginning to understand her a little.

"Giraffe?"

"An animal with a very long neck – see? It comes from Africa," explained Rachel.

But Anne went on looking baffled.

"It's sort of yellow – look – and it has these brown spots."

"Like you," said Rachel. Joanna grabbed a handful of leaves and threw them at her and they burst out laughing. Anne did not like them to fight, but when they laughed she laughed with them.

They gave up on giraffes.

"G for girl, then," said Rachel, drawing one on the page, "if you don't go for giraffes." But Anne, challenged, carefully lettered, G for GIRAF in red pencil across the paper.

Jo and Rachel were delighted. She was learning. She was learning so quickly. They had never done anything so satisfying before.

Today they would not get much beyond the alphabet, but next time they could make a start on one of the books.

Chapter Seven

For the two girls it was beginning to feel like one of those pretending games they used to play when they were much younger.

But this was real.

Wasn't it?

"Perhaps we should tell someone about her," Rachel announced as they walked up the lane. "The people at that school we went to."

"Don't be silly. They won't be there in the holidays. Anyway, I don't think she'd come out if anybody else was around."

"How do you know? She might ... And they could teach her properly – I mean, they had all that equipment, remember? Microphones and stuff."

"You must be crazy! You know where she comes from, same as me!" Joanna sighed. She was beginning to be tired of Rachel's obsession with doing things properly. She didn't want to follow someone else's rules; she wanted to work things out for herself.

But the question of Anne's reality went on bothering Rachel. If she could not be properly helped, she said to herself, then she could not be properly there. Perhaps, in spite of everything, they had really invented Anne. Rachel knew all about inventing people: there had

been, for instance, Philip, her imaginary boy-
friend. Even now, the thought made her
blush.

"You mean she's a ghost," she said crossly,
to cover up for her pink cheeks.

"Don't call her that!" Joanna was furious.
"What do you think we are? To her, I mean."

Rachel was shocked. She hadn't thought of
it like that. Immediately she tested herself for
reality, checking out the weight of the plastic
bag bumping against her leg, the out-of-reach
itch in the middle of her back and the
scratchy texture of the bark as she climbed
the tree. Oh, she was real all right. She felt
angry with Jo.

They were suddenly disliking each other,
but all the same they had something to do.

Sitting as far apart as the branches would
allow, they each separately began to call
Anne.

Anger was something Anne could smell. She
did not need words, sounds, raised voices.

Anger. Irritation. They were tired of
teaching a jolt-head, a beetle-head. She
pointed to herself.

"Anne," she said. "I come not well ..."
and she began to fade.

They protested.

"Oh no," said Rachel. "Don't go."

"It's not you," said Joanna. "It's us. We

had a quarrel but it's over now." Her lips moved too quickly for Anne to read but her gestures were warm and welcoming. They still wanted her.

She remembered the wonderful books and the writing sticks. Not trusting her own memory, she pointed questioningly at the bag.

"Write?" she asked, but when they gave her the exercise books and the crayons, she drew two round faces with down-turned mouths. The two girls giggled self-consciously.

Suddenly Joanna had an idea.

CROSS, she printed, and she stuck out her tongue at Rachel to show what she meant. ANGRY, QUARREL, FIGHT, she wrote. Rachel, catching on, thumbed her nose at Joanna, and between them they pantomimed their quarrel so convincingly that it seemed as if it must have been a joke in the first place.

And Anne, relieved, drew two more faces, this time with smily mouths.

HAPPY, they wrote, and SMILE, stretching their lips with their fingers, waggling their heads and clowning.

ANGRY, copied Anne, and frowned so severely at them that they shrieked with laughter. SMILE, she wrote and grinned at them. Then, watching their faces for approval, she added something of her own.

A MERY PASSUN.

"A merry what?" They listened carefully to

the sounds she was making. A merry pattern? A merry pastime? Rachel worked it out first. "A merry passion? Laughing? Giggling, you mean?" She mimed it and Anne nodded excitedly. "A merry passion!"

Joanna tried it out. "We are in a merry passion," she declared.

"We are very passionate!" Rachel couldn't resist it.

Anne laughed with them. She could not understand their jest, but she knew that their laughter did not exclude her. She could feel their amusement bubbling warmly all round her and it made her want to be part of it.

They had brought things to eat and extra things for Anne. They laid out apples, chocolate bars, three Danish pastries and three bags of crisps. The sight of the little feast made Anne sad. They gave her so much, her two friends, and she could offer them nothing in return. It was not that she hadn't tried. She had brought them fairings — gilded gingerbreads and folded ribbons — but when she came through, she found that her hands were always empty. On her return, she would see her gifts lying in the grass at the base of the sapling.

"Have an apple," said Joanna.

"Wait." Rachel had remembered something from their visit to the school. "Ask for it, Anne. Ask."

Anne was puzzled by this request but she wanted to please them. She asked very politely.

"I prithee let me have it."

The sounds made little sense but the meaning was quite clear. It was very important, Rachel had remembered, for deaf children to communicate, and for other people to listen. Anne had tried.

But when she tried to bite the apple which was, after all, her reward for trying, nothing happened. Her teeth did not even dimple the skin. It was nothing but a jest and she threw it back at them.

Joanna caught it. She was puzzled.

"What's wrong?"

Anne shook her head fiercely. "Not real," she said.

Joanna turned it over and over in her hands. There was nothing wrong with it. It was just an apple. She took a bite out of it and juice ran down her chin.

"It's OK. Look." She handed it back.

Anne tried again but it was like trying to bite into smooth marble. Only then did they realize that she could not eat their food.

Hastily they finished up their snack. It did not taste so good now; they had been looking forward to sharing it with Anne and they had chosen their bits and pieces with great care.

When they brought out the crisps, Anne

screamed. Wood shavings! So they were demons after all. Demons or magicians.

"Wood!" she said. "Wood!" Wood shavings, she thought, and shuddered; a mouthful
of splinters! But no, it was another of their
harmless tricks; why should she care?

"Only crisps," said Joanna.

"Potatoes," said Rachel, scrunching up a
handful of them and offering them for inspec-
tion, but Anne had already gone.

"Frightened by a crisp!"

"It's not funny," Rachel said. "How do we
know she'll come back?"

And when they picked up the exercise book
they saw that all the silly heads had disappeared.

"Look," said Rachel, "everything she's
written, too. All gone."

"It's as if she's not allowed to leave any
marks in our world."

"She can't eat our apples."

"She can't eat any of our stuff, can she?"

"She's just a ghost."

"Don't start that again, Rachel."

"But what's the point?"

"Of what?"

"You know."

"I don't know. We've got to, that's all. I
mean, she remembers things, doesn't she?
And anyway she's a friend and I'm really fond
of her even if you're not."

"But I am. Jo, don't be silly – you know I'm just as fond of her as you are."

"Tomorrow, then."

"OK."

Chapter Eight

It had not been fear which had sent her back.

Even as Anne's fingers closed around the smooth limbs of her sapling, she was thinking that the splintery golden shavings of such alarming appearance were probably nothing more deadly than fritters or thin spice cakes.

No, it had not been fear.

It had been something else.

And she regretted her rude departure, with no proper leave-taking, for she would gladly have tarried with Jo and Rachel, but she seemed to have no choice. For the time she spent in their company was not like ordinary time. It was more like a gift from some good fairy who had supped well from her family's occasional night offerings of bread sops and soured cream. Everyone knew that fairies' gifts were not made to last – that the crock of gold would soon turn back into autumn leaves, and the fat cheese into the yellow face of the moon reflected in a duckpond.

She knew already that she could bring nothing back with her save what remained inside her own head.

But within the blackness of her curtained bed, she could gloat over these treasures which she could not see, practising her words over and over, making letters on paper in her dreams.

Even here, in the byre, she could practise them in secret, while her hands went on pulling rhythmically at the pink teats of the dairy cows. HAPPY. I AM HAPPY. KATERIN IS MOR HAPPY. CROSS. I AM CROSSED. ANGRY. FIGT. I WIL FIGT YOO WIV MI SORD.

Anne's family liked her to be able to perform simple tasks, for that way she could be less of an embarrassment to them. And so she had been taught how to card wool, how to keep the floor rushes fresh with sweet herbs and help the hired women around the farm, for idle hands, they said, even upon one of so little wit, might well be used by the devil. Anne did not mind. She enjoyed milking; she enjoyed being with the slow, patient cows. Their wordless voices, she often felt, ruefully, might not be too unlike her own.

She carried the pails of warm milk into the kitchen and found her sister, Katherine, crimping and decorating a pie, her eyes heavy with secrets, her ring flashing and all the kitchen wenches fluttering around her like doves. Anne watched her cutting little birds out of the pastry, running the point of a knife around a wooden mould. It looked easy — much easier than drawing things on paper — and she wanted to do it, too.

She patted Kate on the shoulder, silently

61

holding out her hand for the knife, but Kate irritably shook herself free. Suddenly Anne could see Rachel's lip-words inside her head: Ask for it, Anne. Ask. Ask ...

Of course.

She put on her best manners.

"I prithee let me try." But nobody listened.

She said it with greater force.

"I prithee, Kate, let me do it." Still no one bothered to listen.

Furious suddenly, she snatched up the knife and carved five letters across the rolled-out paste.

ANGRY

This time Rachel had organized them. She could be quite bossy sometimes but she did get things done. Apples and buns were disposed of long before they called Anne, and when she finally came through, book, pens and crayons were waiting for her in neat little piles.

"More reading today," Rachel announced. She was really enjoying playing teacher.

Anne looked from one to the other. Yesterday they had seemed like two strangers who didn't like each other very much. Today the warmth of their friendship enclosed her like a soft woollen shawl.

"A better humour," she remarked boldly, for the morning's happenings had made her bold, but when she saw that they did not understand what she meant, she said, "Happy. No more strife," and they grinned at each other sheepishly.

Then Joanna opened the book. It was a new one, and they were rather pleased with it. Feeling that some of the others were a bit tatty, they had pooled their pocket money and bought a cheap reading primer.

The first part consisted of nothing but games: things like matching shapes and finding two identical mice or sheep or tortoises in a row. They felt a bit embarrassed presenting such infantile stuff to someone of their own age, but Anne was fascinated. Next, they got her to crayon over dotted-line letters. Already she recognized most of them, so she tried, instead, to make them beautiful, choosing her colours with great care.

Then came a story with pictures.

"Look," said Joanna, and she read aloud, pointing to each word. "'The old woman made a gingerbread man.'" She took pains to pronounce the sentence very carefully.

And Anne read the words, looked at the picture for confirmation, and understood.

"'The gingerbread man ran away,'" read Joanna. "'The gingerbread man saw a horse.'"

Anne's eyes sparkled when she saw the horse and she held up three fingers.

"Three?" said Rachel, feeling slightly envious. "One, two, three?" And Anne nodded. "You lucky thing!"

"'He saw a cat.'"

Anne looked pleased. She held up four fingers this time: she was really showing off.

"Four cats?" said Joanna, and Anne nodded.

"Mice," she said. "Mice. And rats." To show them what she meant, she drew a collection of them with black whiskers and long, wiggly tails. Then she remembered something.

"Mine," she said. "Meg."

She pointed at Joanna's hair.

"A ginger cat? Carrots? Like her?"

Anne nodded.

Then she pointed at her own white cap, and patted her chest.

"White? White, too?" They were enjoying the guessing game.

"A white shirt-front!" shrieked Joanna.

"Stick," demanded Anne, reaching out for a felt tip. Then she remembered her manners. "I prithee ..." and she drew a cat and coloured it orange, leaving the white bits on its chest and paws. Underneath the drawing, she carefully printed MEG, and got it right.

"We've got a cat," said Joanna. "He's called Fred." She drew a silly-looking cat in black crayon, leaving out the white bits as Anne had done and wrote FRED underneath it. Then as an afterthought, she added, A BOY. She pointed out a boy in the book. Then she pointed to the three of them.

"Girls."

Anne nodded wisely.

"Babes," she said, pointing to her own stomach. "Soon."

"What?" Joanna was horrified.

"Silly! She means Meg. Meg's pregnant."

"Ooh, kittens!" said Joanna, feeling a little foolish.

They got back to the lesson, and turned to a page of sentences, each one beginning with "Here is a".

"'Here is a ...'"

Anne looked at the picture. "Tree!" she shouted triumphantly.

"Write it," said Rachel.

They tried the next one.

"'Here is a ...'"

"Bauble!"

"No, silly, it's a ball. A b–a–l–l. Anne. Write it!"

"'Here is a ...'"

It was a house, if they said so. Apart from the chimney pot, it was nothing like any house Anne had ever seen, but she wrote it down obediently HERE IS A HOUSE.

"'Here is a ...'" They should have missed this one out, but it was the next sentence and they were trapped.

"Car," said Joanna, before she could stop herself.

"What . . . ?"

They did some quick thinking.

"A chariot," said Rachel.

"Don't be daft!" said Jo. "A coach, Anne. It's like a coach."

"But it doesn't have any horses."

They were talking nonsense. She could read some of their words but she could make no kind of sense out of what they were saying. A coat was something to wear; this small, lozenge-shaped object looked like a painted bead, and what horses had to do with it all left her quite speechless.

She was still trying to work it all out, frowning, as she walked back through the meadow.

Rachel sighed.

"Oh, well . . ."

"We did lots, though, didn't we?"

"Almost half the book."

"She learns really quickly."

"But nothing stays. I mean, all her funny drawings and those coloured letters she did – they all go away. She can't even take them back with her to show her mum."

"Maybe her mum doesn't care that much . . . maybe she's a bit embarrassed by her . . . I mean, her voice is funny and she can't hear anything anyone says."

"Well, she's got a cat. And three horses . . . Things can't be that bad."

Chapter Nine

The lessons were becoming almost a routine.

Although they could not share their secret with anyone (for who would believe them?) it was beginning to seem perfectly natural to go along two or three times a week to teach a deaf girl from another century to read and write. Of course, they never did express it quite like that or they might have started doubting themselves. She was Anne, simply Anne; she was their friend and they loved her dearly. They were so fond of her that they were gradually allowing her to become an extension of that close friendship which had started five years ago when they first sat next to each other at Infants' school. Instead of two of them, now there were three – Rachel, Jo and Anne.

But it was not always easy.

One of the frustrating things about it was that, outside the tree itself, Anne appeared to have no existence in their world at all. They longed to take her home with them sometimes and share more things with her but they could not. And their respective families seemed so remote, like an ongoing legend which they could only imagine.

"I'd swap my brother for you, Anne," said Jo one afternoon after Mark had been particularly irritating.

Anne frowned. "Swap?"

"Exchange. Give."

Anne's face lit up.

"My sister Kate." And so well did she mime her sister Kate that they could almost see her there, fussing over the set of her lace collar, polishing her betrothal ring against her petticoats and admiring the blue glitter of the stones, delicately tweaking at a raised eyebrow with little grimaces of pain and rehearsing all her coy glances in a hand-held mirror.

Not to be outdone, Jo took the exercise book and drew quite a good caricature of Mark with his exaggerated, gelled hairstyle.

Below it, she printed, HERE IS MY BROTHER MARK. She hesitated, wondering how to turn "He is an arrogant creep" into the sort of words Anne would understand. Finally she added, HE IS PROUD AND FOOLISH.

Anne grinned and reached out for the pencils – it was her turn. She drew them a picture of Kate in all her betrothal finery, with her stiff high ruff and with an outsize ring on her finger.

HERE IS MY SISTER KATE, she wrote very carefully. She paused. Then she added, SHE IS TOO CUMLY.

Now it was their turn.

"Cumly?"

Anne traced the oval of her face with her fingertip, and simpered.

"Vain?"

Anne shook her head.

"Proud?" It was still not quite right. "Pretty? Attractive? Beautiful?"

Anne nodded vigorously. "Yes, yes."

"But you are very – cumly – too," Rachel protested.

Anne, amazed, blushed and turned away, for no one had ever said that of her.

She stood on tiptoe and examined her reflection in the small round mirror on the wall. Anne? Comely?

Fool she had often been called, and lackwit and sometimes Anne-the-Curst when she railed against that wall of silence which cut her off, not only from other people but even from the sound of her own fury. But comely?

And yet . . .

These days Anne moved with a different step. Even her father had noticed it.

"Why, the child has a little grace after all," he said wonderingly.

And each day she worked at her writing, making the letters wherever she could – with a stick on the bare earth, with chalk on the flagstones, or the dark beams or red bricks of the house – until finally, exasperated, they cut her a quill and found her an old, wine-stained ledger for her scribblings.

Rachel and Joanna were uneasy.

Their spare time was being increasingly gobbled up by activities to do with their new school. Although term would not start for another week or two, the First Years were invited to an Open Day so that they could get to know the layout of the buildings.

Rachel's mum pinned up the school checklist and ticked off each item as they bought it.

Joanna's mum lost hers and they had a screaming row about it. "Who cares anyway?" said Mark. "Don't need half the junk they tell you to get."

They went together to a pre-term sale of school uniform and Jo's mum, who made up stuffed toys for a factory, took in seams and turned up hems so that the things fitted the two girls perfectly.

They had a dress rehearsal.

"Trendy!" sneered Mark.

"Oh, shut up!" said Joanna, but Rachel just giggled.

Jo put her name on the waiting list for the School Drama Club.

Rachel, who already played recorder in a music group, signed on for flute lessons.

It was scary but exciting, waiting for the beginning of the new term.

But Anne . . .

What was going to happen when the new term did start and they could only get to the park at weekends?

They tried talking to her about it but they could not get her to understand. School? That was only for boys. Rachel and Joanna imagined things must have been very different in Elizabethan times but they didn't really know.

And you grew up more quickly then, they supposed.

They thought about Kate, who was only fifteen and soon to be married. There were times when, compared with Anne, they felt like children.

Chapter Ten

Anne wondered if they were still her friends, for they had come less frequently of late. And even when they were sitting beside her in the tree, they seemed ... different.

For in the last few days, they had begun to take on a sort of transparency – almost as if they were ghosts. She did not want them to be ghosts: she refused to believe that they were. Ghosts did not have red hair tied up in bunches. Ghosts did not blush. And you could not play games with a ghost, or giggle so much that you nearly fell out of the tree. Oh, Anne knew what ghosts were like: they had skulls instead of heads and they frightened people.

Rachel and Jo did not frighten her. They were real. They were her friends and she wanted to stay with them. If she could have chosen, she would have stayed with them for ever.

She loved them so much.

And since their appearance, on that magical afternoon, her life had changed and she had no desire for it to change back. She was no longer prepared to be the family lackwit, the poor imbecile, the fool.

She was no fool – she knew that now.

She could write her name. She could read

letters.

She was Anne.

Hopefully, she ran her fingers over the sapling oak. At last, she felt the girls calling her, "Anne ... Anne ... Where are you? Come out and play." But now the call was so weak that she could scarcely feel it.

And the space through which she looked to find her two friends was no longer clear but like a muddy pool and, even when she passed over it, things still appeared as blurred and smudged as a mummers' painted scenecloth after a shower. Even the thick, solid branch on which she was sitting felt light and insubstantial, as if it had been made out of paste and gauze.

The others had noticed the difference, too.

"Oh, Anne," said Joanna, squinting, "you've gone all funny."

Well, so had they, but Anne did not want to think about it. For the faces of her two friends had already begun to drift and melt, like reflections in troubled water, but they were still there and that was all that mattered.

And she had so many things to tell them. She took a deep breath; she had been holding her news all morning and now she could say it.

"Kitlings," she announced proudly. Earlier that day, she had come across Meg's new babies stumbling around blindly in the yellow straw of the barn.

But the girls did not seem to understand.

After she had said the word over and over again she lost patience with them, so she reached for a pen and drew a mother cat with five tiny cats sitting beside her in a row.

"Oh, kittens!" they shrieked.

And Anne vanished.

She could feel herself going and she was furious.

She had spent only minutes with them. It wasn't fair. She panicked and grabbed at things – branches, twigs, leaves, even – but it was like grasping at air.

Anne was gone.

She had stayed for such a short time. They hadn't even started her lesson. What was wrong? Had they said something to upset her?

For about ten minutes, Rachel and Joanna sat there numbly, refusing to believe that Anne would not, at any moment, reappear, with some incomprehensible explanation, even though she had never done such a thing before. They tried calling her again, screwing up their faces with concentration, but there was no response. They had always known when she was coming because of the feeling of tension, the slight tingling in the air around them. Now there was nothing. Nothing at all.

At last they gave up. And there seemed to be no point in hanging around, so they packed their things and climbed down.

All the way home they kept asking each other if it had been something they had said or something they had done. Was it because they had not understood her funny word for kittens? Was she offended? Had they hurt her feeelings by being simply two more people who couldn't understand what she was trying to say?

"Perhaps it was just too much for her," said Joanna.

"But she was learning so quickly!"

"Look," said Jo. "Let's leave it for a week. Give her time to digest it all – I mean, imagine learning to read and write at our age. It must be a bit of a shock."

It was over.

Anne knew it.

She had always known that the fairies' gift was bound to wear thin and been aware that the time she was allowed to spend in that enchanted place was limited. But now, suddenly, there was no time left and she knew that she would never see Rachel and Joanna again.

She began to cry. It had been a cruel jest to offer her the things she wanted most, only to snatch them away. She kicked at the sapling. Who wanted a sapling? She wanted the big tree. She wanted her friends.

And the very thought of going back to the house appalled her. She would never go back. She would stay here, in the woods. She would become an outlaw or a wild woman.

When it grew late, Katherine said, "But where is Anne?"

They searched the house, the garden, the barns and the byres but there was no sign of her.

At last, in desperation, they began to look for her in the fringes of the forest.

They did not have to look far.

There she was, lying under a young tree, clutching at handfuls of nothing at all and sobbing her heart out. Her mind, they could clearly see, had gone at last. She had finally lost even that modest half a wit with which they had so grudgingly credited her. Mistress Latymer thought of the lunatics in the Bedlam Hospital and shuddered. Not that, she thought. She is, after all, my daughter, my own child.

They pulled Anne to her feet and tried to talk some sense into her, but she would have none of it. Crying like a baby, she fought them, tugging at Kate's hair and pushing her mother away. And all the time she was babbling, in that strange, animal tongue out of which they could sometimes pick the odd word or two, some nonsense about a Jo and a Rachel. But there was no Joseph in Finchley village and the only Rachel was a wanton wench and no fit company for Anne.

Inside the house she broke free, but when she found that they had locked the doors, she hid herself in a store cupboard.

"Nay, let her be," said Mistress Latymer. "Let her cool her heels and her passions. In quiet her reason may be restored."

"A sound whipping might restore it faster," muttered one of the hired women, for it was well known in the village that Philip Latymer was far too mild when it came to family discipline.

And down in the kitchen, they shook their heads in despair.

"The maid has a devil in her," they said. "Far better if she had never been born."

Joanna and Rachel spent a great deal of the following week preparing Anne's next lesson.

This time, they considered very carefully how much they should teach her, and how long each lesson should be. And they resolved to try even harder to understand all the things she was saying, for each of them knew how awful it felt not to be understood.

They also resolved not to get too excited or giggly when she was with them.

Maybe Anne was not used to that sort of thing.

For a whole day, Anne lay with her face turned to the wall, saying nothing and scarcely moving, as if she were grieving for someone lost.

They had sometimes seen young widows in this sort of state, but never a child.

And Katherine and Mistress Latymer picked armfuls of rosemary and pulled up garlic bulbs and hung them in bunches around her bed, so that the heavy curtains began to smell more of the kitchen than a bedchamber. And they brought in a priest to help them pray. They prayed that the evil spirits which had so clearly possessed her should depart, for she was not too young to be hanged as a witch and, in their own, odd way, they were fond of her.

The herbs were effective and the prayers were heard.

Anne recovered.

But after that, they kept a careful watch over her, not letting her stray far from the house, for who could say what evil she might have met with in the forest?

One day, her mother found her making letters in the old ledger. She was amazed at Anne's bold penstrokes.

"If you must write, then you shall!" she

79

declared with sudden determination. "There are those who would say I am half-crazed myself to do it and I don't know who will teach you, but we will find you a tutor. And praise the Lord you have a little wit."

On the following Monday, Joanna and Rachel went back to the tree with their collection of books and pens and pencils and all their good intentions.

They climbed up to the attic branch and waited.

They waited for a long time, but nothing happened. There was no feeling of being watched, no tingling in the air, nothing. Nothing but the hum of distant traffic and the yelling of little kids playing.

"Let's concentrate, then," said Jo at last. "Let's start calling her like we used to."

So they each closed their eyes and thought about Anne. They thought about her pale face and her dark, frightened eyes. They remembered her thin, nervous fingers shyly twisting a loop of fabric in her long skirt. And they remembered her smile, and her funny, funny voice.

Come out, Anne, they thought. Come out. Come out and play with us. We love you ...

But when they opened their eyes, all they could see were flakes of blue sky between brown-scalloped, rustling oak leaves. Sunlight suddenly flickered silver and, for a moment, they were convinced that something was happening, but nothing did.

They tried again and again, with increasing hopelessness; they did not really expect her to come, and she did not.

Towards the end of the afternoon, they felt the lower branches of the tree shaking violently. Anne ... it had to be. They waited, crossing their fingers and holding their breath.

At last, two grubby faces appeared through the leaves.

"Get out of our tree," shouted one of the boys, "or we'll bash you!"

And without another word, they left.

Chapter Eleven

They found her a teacher, and life, for Anne, slowly changed.

For even if she could not say words properly, she could write them. Best of all, she liked writing her own name – ANNE – and decorating it with squiggles and flourishes. And she insisted on cutting the quills herself, picking out the very best goose feathers and carefully slitting and shaping the ends.

When her family saw this unexpected eagerness for learning, they offered her, out of curiosity, more. Secretly, they were beginning to feel quite proud of Anne. She was becoming almost an asset – and a performing pet was, after all, easier to live with than a gibbering idiot. They set her to sew and embroider with the women, and marvelled – to Anne's fury – at every stitch she placed accurately upon the linen. Her father, somewhat unwillingly, tried teaching her to add figures together. In future years he would turn more and more towards this once-rejected daughter, even asking for her help when his accounts would not make sense.

Now when people made jests about her daughter's speech, Mistress Latymer would chide them.

"My Anne makes more sense than many I

could name in this household," she would retort.

And she began to boast of Anne's prowess to the women.

"Anne's no fool," she would declare proudly. "She can read and write with the best of them. Of course," she would take good care to add, "it is to be expected, for she comes of excellent stock."

Rachel and Joanna went on trying.

They tried the next day and the day after that, closing their eyes and concentrating, calling Anne, Anne ... but nothing happened.

Nothing ever happened and they began to feel a bit silly. The whole thing was becoming a bore. Anyway, the holidays were nearly over and there were more important things to be thinking about, like the big, slightly scary new school. Perhaps it had all been nothing but a summer fantasy which had run away with them.

Just before the new term started, Rachel organized her things and tidied up her room. When she came across the alphabet book, she threw it into the dustbin and the picture books she dumped in a bag to take back to Oxfam.

One day, Anne decided to make herself a

sampler.

And why not, said her mother.

A waste of money, some of the women muttered. Materials were expensive and it was family wealth squandered on the whims of a poor fool – she should be well content with the scraps and remnants she was given. But these days, Mistress Latymer listened to no one.

The linen was purchased and set up on a small frame and Anne's mother showed her how to catch it to the webbing so that it could be stretched. She picked out the silks. Yellow, the child had asked for, and brown, holding a marigold against a scrap of brown velvet, to show them exactly what she wanted. And scarlet and mauve.

And a fine waste of money it was turning out to be, whatever Mistress Latymer might say to the contrary. The women could see quite clearly that Anne's head was still stuffed full of sick fancies, for no beast, neither heraldic nor natural, could possibly be as distorted as the creature she was making. And besides, no one with any understanding of how such things were done, would ruin the symmetry of the piece by extending the neck of the beast up into the neat bands of stitch-patterns and the little garlands of flowers.

But Anne did not give a fig for what they thought. She was making it for herself.

The women watched, with benevolent amusement, as the design grew. The animal's face, for instance, with the grin of a man, could only, surely, have grown out of a fevered imagination. The child had even drawn in her own name – such wanton pride! – and was carefully filling in the letters with small satin stitches. In short, it was not the least like anyone else's sampler, but then, what could you expect of a child like Anne?

Anne took great pains over the words, lovingly making each letter. Her friends would be proud of her, she thought wistfully.

She missed them ...

Many times, when people were looking the other way, she had sneaked out to the forest. She wanted, at least, to thank them.

But each time, the sapling remained a sapling, no matter how much she willed it to grow, and the only big, old trees were the ones which had always been there. And already they were beginning to seem like a dream, the two girls in the tree, but it was a dream much too precious to lose. She wanted to hold it in some way, preserve it for herself for ever.

The work was nearly finished. There was just enough room.

Standing at the embroidery frame, she stitched in the two small figures in their blue hose, with the tiny tree beside them. And above them, all brown-spotted and glorious in yellow, straddled the wonderful Giraf animal, pushing its neck boldly into the flowers, and smiling, as she remembered it smiling in the bestiary.

Now it was told.

Chapter Twelve

It was an icy afternoon in mid-February. Outside in the street, the bare branches of the plane trees were dangling their dark, frozen fruit against a cold blue sky.

Inside the museum, Rachel had dutifully covered three pages of her exercise book with notes and sketches and now she was restless. One or two people were fooling about; others had gone wandering off in search of Coke, crisps, postcards or lavatories.

Down behind the last display case, Joanna was doodling over the project title INVESTIGATING HISTORY – illuminating it with orange and pink felt-tip. She sighed. What a boring teacher! What a boring afternoon! What a boring way to spend a couple of hours in the middle of town. She considered, for a moment, investigating the windows of the tantalizing shops up the road, but Miss O'Connor had said four o'clock at the main entrance and there simply wasn't enough time.

These days, the two girls did not see nearly as much of each other. Ever since Jo had been given a tiny, walk-on part in the school pantomime, she had become totally hooked on acting, and Rachel, with a secret crush on someone in the Junior Orchestra, kept staying behind for extra flute practice.

Last summer was a half-forgotten dream — something to do with leaving Primary school, something to do with a childhood they were both outgrowing.

Joanna, restless, decided to wander.

On her way out, she spotted Rachel.

"Come for a coffee?" said Jo.

"No chance." Rachel pointed at the plastic-wrapped scroll sticking out of her bag. "No money. Bought one of those posters."

"Oh well," said Jo. "In that case I'll find the Costume Court and look at some clothes."

"You would. I'll come with you."

They turned right and wandered vaguely up the main staircase.

"This where it is?"

"What?"

"Costume Court, stupid."

"Not sure," said Jo. "I lost my map."

"You can borrow mine if you like."

This irritated Jo and she immediately changed the subject.

"What's down there?"

"Let's find out."

It was pottery, which was a bore, but further along and round a corner there were little rooms they could look into, each one furnished in the style of a different century.

"Look at that chair!"

"Imagine living in a place like that."

They lingered over the Elizabethan room with its heavily curtained bed.

"Imagine sleeping in that thing – you'd get nightmares."

But Jo was staring at the portrait that hung above the linen chest.

"Maybe she ..." She stopped herself quickly. "She's got problems," she said loudly, moving away to point at a shiny porcelain nymph with yellow hair and a sorrowful expression.

"What sort of problems?"

"Spare tyre – look! And look at her stomach." There was no one watching so she ran her finger over the cold curve. "Needs a good diet!"

They began to giggle.

A uniformed attendant appeared unexpectedly from round the corner – a solemn young man built like a wrestler.

Joanna grabbed Rachel's arm.

"Quick!" she whispered. "Up there."

They clattered up the stairs. It suddenly felt good to be doing something together again, something secret and mildly silly – a bit like that old tree game they didn't talk about any more.

"Blimey!" said Rachel.

"Him Tarzan! Me Jo," muttered Joanna, beating her chest with her fists, and they started giggling again.

They seemed to have the whole place to themselves up there in those dimly-lit galleries, where the white glitter of winter sunlight was softened by canvas blinds to a honeyed gold. But soon the silence became too much for them.

Jo started fooling around.

She reared up, waving her arms.

"Me Tarzan!" she announced, leaping about and scratching her armpits. "Watch out! I'm coming to get you!"

It was a perfect place for hide and seek, with its rows and rows of tall wooden frames on polished chests.

Rachel squealed and ran, ducking into one of the aisles.

Joanna waited, listening.

The silence returned.

Then Rachel snorted.

"I heard that," called Joanna.

She started to weave in and out between the aisles, but Rachel had cleverly slipped away and was already creeping up on her from the other side.

Baffled for a moment, Jo began fiddling with the wooden frames.

"Hey, Rache," she said, looking in the wrong direction.

Rachel jumped out at her, grabbing her round the shoulders, "Got you!" she said.

"They come out," said Jo, shaking her off. "Look ..."

The frames held pieces of embroidery displayed under glass. Jo showed Rachel how each piece could be pulled out by its wooden handle and looked at.

"Oh, yes," said Rachel.

So for a while, they amused themselves by browsing through the pieces, dreamily pushing them in and out without really looking at them. The silence closed around them again. Suddenly they wanted to talk in whispers. It was so very peaceful ... it was as if they had all the time in the world; it was as if the whole museum had become their own private attic.

"Oh look at these," said Rachel.

Jo read the label.

"Sixteenth century." She felt excited, which was funny. Dates, apart from birthdays, did not usually interest her.

"You see?" said Rachel. "So we don't need to look anywhere else, do we?" She had no idea why she had said that.

And at once they began to flip out the frames, one after another, like a huge and heavy pack of cards, aware that they were looking for something, but pretending, all the time, that they were not; giggling nervously and making flippant remarks as if it were still a game.

Samplers. Just bands of white stitches over off-white linen. Well, fine, if you were a needlework teacher. Fine, if you liked that sort of thing, but they did not. Samplers with coloured flowers. Well, those were a bit more inspiring. They picked out pansies and honeysuckle, roses and daffodils.

"Funny," said Jo, without thinking, "that the same flowers were around when . . ."

"When Queen Elizabeth was on the throne?" Rachel said quickly. "Yes, it is, isn't it?"

Samplers with beasts — now, they were more fun. Lions and unicorns, porcupines and rabbits, serpents, dogs and cats, butterflies, and even a caterpillar. But so what? Nice animal pictures you could find in any library. Better ones than these. It was a long time ago, the sixteenth century. It had nothing at all to do with Rachel and Joanna.

"But we still haven't found it," said Rachel.

"Found what?"

"Oh," and Rachel went very pink, "dunno. You know . . ."

After this pointless conversation, they were ready to give up. Then one of the frames caught Jo's attention.

"Wait a minute," she said.

Slowly, she pulled it out.

They looked.

It was quite a small sampler and very worn

at the edges, but there was something about it that bothered them, something that did not quite fit.

They read the label. It was difficult to understand.

> COLOURED SILKS IN SATIN, HOLBEIN, CROSS, BUTTON-HOLE, ALGERIAN EYE, RUSSIAN DRAWN AND OVERCAST FILLING STITCHES ON LINEN BASE. A VERY RECENT ACQUISITION AND SOMETHING OF A CURIOSITY. THE GIRAFFE MOTIF WOULD SUGGEST A MUCH LATER PERIOD, BUT THE NAME AND DATE (AGAIN, RARELY FOUND IN SAMPLERS AT THIS TIME) ARE UNDOUBTEDLY GENUINE.

A giraffe.

They had not immediately recognized the faded, yellow and brown animal in the centre of the sampler, but now they could clearly see its quite exceptional neck poking incongruously through the uneven bands of roses and violas, and its silly face smiling its ridiculous smile.

THIS EXTRAORDINARY IMAGE, they read, COULD ALMOST HAVE COME OUT OF A MODERN CHILD'S PICTURE BOOK.

"Oh," said Rachel.

"Really," said Joanna.

Then they spotted the two little figures with blue legs, standing beside a tiny tree. And the hair of one had been worked in bright yellow silk and the hair of the other in red.

And across the bottom, with careful stitches, the maker had embroidered her own name.

ANNE LATYMER. AGED ELEVEN.
ANNO DOMINI 1598.